Movie Madness

Don't miss a single

Nancy Drew
Clue Book:

Pool Party Puzzler

Last Lemonade Standing

A Star Witness

Big Top Flop

Nancy Drew
* CLUE BOOK *
#5

Movie Madness

BY CAROLYN KEENE * ILLUSTRATED BY PETER FRANCIS

Aladdin
NEW YORK   LONDON   TORONTO   SYDNEY   NEW DELHI

This book is a work of fiction. Any references to historical events, real people, or real places are used fictitiously. Other names, characters, places, and events are products of the author's imagination, and any resemblance to actual events or places or persons, living or dead, is entirely coincidental.

ALADDIN

An imprint of Simon & Schuster Children's Publishing Division
1230 Avenue of the Americas, New York, NY 10020
First Aladdin paperback edition July 2016
Text copyright © 2016 by Simon & Schuster, Inc.
Illustrations copyright © 2016 by Peter Francis
Also available in an Aladdin hardcover edition.
ALADDIN is a trademark of Simon & Schuster, Inc., and related logo
is a registered trademark of Simon & Schuster, Inc.
NANCY DREW, NANCY DREW CLUE BOOK, and colophons
are registered trademarks of Simon & Schuster, Inc.
All rights reserved, including the right of reproduction in whole or in part in any form.
For information about special discounts for bulk purchases, please contact
Simon & Schuster Special Sales at 1-866-506-1949 or business@simonandschuster.com.
The Simon & Schuster Speakers Bureau can bring authors to your live event.
For more information or to book an event contact the Simon & Schuster Speakers Bureau
at 1-866-248-3049 or visit our website at www.simonspeakers.com.
Designed by Karina Granda
The illustrations for this book were rendered digitally.
The text of this book was set in Adobe Garamond Pro.
Manufactured in the United States of America 0616 OFF
2 4 6 8 10 9 7 5 3 1
Library of Congress Control Number 2016939794
ISBN 978-1-4814-5821-4 (hc)
ISBN 978-1-4814-5820-7 (pbk)
ISBN 978-1-4814-5822-1 (eBook)

* CONTENTS *

Chapter

PICTURE PERFECT

"How lucky are we to be living in Hollywood, you guys?" eight-year-old Bess Marvin asked excitedly.

Nancy Drew and George Fayne stopped walking to stare at Bess. Did she just say . . . Hollywood?

"Bess, we don't live in Hollywood," Nancy insisted. "We live in River Heights."

"Huge difference!" George pointed out.

"I know!" Bess agreed with a toss of her long

blond hair. "But a movie is about to be filmed right here. That makes River Heights practically Hollywood, right?"

"I guess!" Nancy said with a smile.

All three best friends had reason to smile: Summer vacation had just begun. Even better, a scene in the next Glam Girl action-adventure movie would be filmed right in their own neighborhood at Turtle Shell Playground!

"I still can't believe they're using kids from the neighborhood as movie extras!" Nancy said as they headed for the playground.

"Being in a movie will be cool," George admitted. "I just don't get why Glam Girl is so special."

"Are you serious, George?" Bess gasped. "Glam Girl is the only fashion-forward superhero who gets her powers from clothes!"

"A pair of sunglasses gives Glam Girl X-ray vision!" Nancy explained. "A hat lets her read minds, and gloves give her power to point and freeze any villain in his or her tracks!"

"Don't forget Glam Girl's electric-blue hair!"

Bess said excitedly. "How awesome is that?"

"Sure, if you're a Smurf!" George snorted.

"Here's something awesome," Nancy added. "Shasta Sienna, the actress who plays Glam Girl, says she does all her own stunts—like jumping out of planes and off of speeding trains!"

"Stunts are cool," Bess said, "but I'm more interested in the clothes Glam Girl will wear in this movie."

George twisted one of her dark curls happily. "I'm interested in the special effects. Practically all movie special effects are computerized!"

"Computers, clothes—are you sure you're cousins?" Nancy asked Bess and George. "You're as different as—"

"River Heights and Hollywood!" George finished.

Bess was a serious fashionista with a room full of clothes and accessories. The only fashion accessory George dreamed of was a smartwatch!

"Speaking of movies," George said. "Look at who's up the block."

Nancy glanced ahead to see their classmate Sidney Schacter standing on his toes and taping a flier to a tree. Sidney was a major movie fanboy. He had even started his own movie-loving club called "Popcorn Peeps."

"Hi, Sidney," Nancy said as they walked over. "Are you going to be an extra in the Glam Girl movie today?"

"Nope," Sidney said. "I'd rather work on this!"

Sidney pointed proudly to the flier and said, "The Popcorn Peeps' first awesome movie museum in the basement of my house!"

"A real-live museum?" Bess asked.

"What's in it so far?" Nancy wanted to know.

"Only the most excellent movie memorabilia," Sidney said. "We've got a wad of gum that was chewed and spit out by a top-secret superstar celeb, an autographed pizza-parlor napkin with another star's lipstick stain—"

"And gross grease stains, too, I'm sure," Bess cut in.

"Gross to some . . . awesome to others," Sidney said. "Come to our museum on opening day and see for yourselves."

Bess shook her head. "If you want kids to visit your museum, Sidney, you need better stuff than a wad of gum and a greasy napkin."

"Maybe you can get something from Shasta Sienna on the Glam Girl set today," Nancy suggested.

"Maybe she'll spit out her gum!" George joked.

"Har-har," Sidney said, pretending to laugh. "What do you know about movies, anyway? Aren't you detectives?"

"The best!" Bess declared. "We have our own detective club called the Clue Crew."

"I know that," Sidney said.

"Nancy even has a Clue Book where she writes down all our clues and suspects," George went on. "Right, Nancy?"

"Right, but today these detectives are going to be movie stars," Nancy said. "So we'd better get going."

"Good luck with your museum, Sidney," Bess said with a little wave good-bye.

Sidney nodded thanks, but as the girls walked away, he seemed deep in thought.

"Maybe he'll take your advice about getting something from Shasta, Nancy," George said.

"Something less gross!" Bess added with a frown.

When the girls reached Turtle Shell Playground, they couldn't believe their eyes. Their favorite swings, slides, and monkey bars were surrounded by movie cameras and trailers. Microphones called "boom mikes" were attached to long poles that were carried by staff wearing headsets. Other crew members also wearing headsets and Glam Girl T-shirts scurried about busily.

"Are you sure this is our playground?" Nancy gasped with surprise.

A woman with a smile walked over. The name on her ID tag read KEISHA ELLIOT.

"If you girls are here to be extras," Keisha explained, "you can hand in your permission slips at that table over there."

Nancy turned to see more kids lined up at the table. They looked just as excited as she was!

"Excuse me," Bess asked politely, "but what clothes will give Glam Girl her special powers in this movie?"

"Boots!" Keisha replied. "They will give Glam Girl the power to run superfast and jump superhigh."

"My sneakers do that." George sighed.

"George, be nice!" Bess hissed.

The girls hurried to the table. They stood

behind a girl with long curly hair. Nancy recognized the girl as Paloma Garva from the fourth grade at school.

Paloma's hair was perfectly brushed and styled. Her yellow sandals perfectly matched her sundress, and her toenails were perfectly polished. That's because Paloma was the school perfectionist—and proud of it!

"The way they're doing this is all wrong!" Paloma said with a groan when she saw the girls. "If they had us line up in alphabetical order, it would be so much more perfect!"

"I guess you want to be a movie extra too, huh, Paloma?" George asked.

"Only if I'm offered the perfect part," Paloma remarked, "like Glam Girl's little sister or something."

"If you're Glam Girl's sister, you might have to dye your hair blue!" Bess pointed out.

Paloma's eyes widened. "No way! I'm in a huge fashion show tomorrow. It's at a new store at the mall called Girly Gear."

"I heard about that store," Nancy said.

"Not me," George insisted. "I don't do girly."

"We know," Bess said with a sigh as she frowned at her cousin's sweatpants and T-shirt.

"What will you be modeling, Paloma?" Nancy asked.

"They gave me the perfect outfit," Paloma boasted. "All I need is the perfect pair of blue shoes to match—"

"OMG!" Bess cut in with a gasp. "Look!"

"Is it Glam Girl?" Nancy asked as she turned to see where Bess was pointing.

"Better!" Bess exclaimed. "Her boots!"

Nancy, Bess, and Paloma raced toward a young man carrying a pair of boots on a silver tray. George groaned as she lagged behind.

"Are those Glam Girl's boots?" Bess asked the man. "The ones she'll wear in the movie?"

The man, whose ID tag read MATT MCCABE, gripped the tray tightly as he replied, "Yes, they are."

Nancy brushed aside her reddish-blond bangs

to see the boots. They were blue boots with a strip of shiny yellow fabric at the tops.

"So pretty!" Nancy swooned. But just as she pointed to the boots, Matt pulled the tray back.

"No touching, please," Matt insisted. "They're custom-made for Shasta Sienna's feet."

"Wrong!" Paloma said as she stepped closer to the tray. "These boots were made for *me*!"

Nancy gasped as Paloma grabbed Glam Girl's boots off the tray. What was Paloma doing?

Chapter

SHOCK-BUSTER MOVIE

"Thank you!" Paloma said as she held one boot in each hand. "These boots are the perfect blue for my Girly Gear fashion-show outfit!"

"You won't fit into them, Paloma," Nancy said. "They're grown-up boots!"

"Ladies size six, which is Shasta's shoe size," Matt told Paloma. "Now put them back, or you'll never work in this town again!"

"I'm too young to work," Paloma scoffed. She then smiled lovingly at the boots. "But I am totally going to work these perfect boots!"

"You guys!" George exclaimed. "Here comes Shasta!"

"Shasta? Omigosh, where?" Paloma cried.

As Paloma turned her head, George snatched the boots from Paloma's hands.

"Score!" George said, holding up the boots high.

"Sneaky trick, Georgia Fayne!" Paloma snapped.

Nancy could see George cringe as she plunked the boots back on the tray. George hated her real name, Georgia, more than broccoli-flavored jelly beans!

"Who wants to be in this dumb movie, anyway?" Paloma grumbled as she huffed away. "I am so outta here!"

"Buh-bye," Matt called as he carried the blue boots in another direction. "Thanks for your help, Georgia!"

"It's George," she muttered through gritted teeth. "And you're welcome." They were about to head back to the table when George pointed and said, "Look! There's Glam Girl!"

Bess rolled her eyes. "You don't have to pull that trick on *us*, George. We didn't take any boots."

But then Nancy saw a flash of bright blue in the distance. It was Glam Girl's famous blue hair! And that meant . . .

"It's Glam Girl!" Nancy exclaimed.

Nancy, Bess, and George raced after the superhero. She turned sharply behind a big silver trailer. On the door of the trailer were a star and the name, SHASTA SIENNA.

George was the first to reach the trailer and peek behind it.

"Do you see Glam Girl, George?" Bess whispered.

"No," George whispered back. "I see two Glam Girls!"

"Two Glam Girls?" Nancy cried.

She and Bess peeked too. Just as George had said, two Glam Girls stood face-to-face behind the trailer.

One shook her head in disbelief while saying,

"I'm your stunt double, Shasta. Why do I have to hide?"

"Because everyone thinks I do my own stunts, Rosie," Shasta replied. "You have to hide before the kids see you."

Nancy couldn't believe her ears. Shasta had claimed to do all her own stunts!

Suddenly—

"Ouch!" Bess cried as a mosquito bit her wrist.

Both Glam Girls' heads turned to see Nancy, Bess, and George peeking from the front of the trailer.

"Oops," Rosie said with a smile. "Looks like your secret is out, Shasta."

Shasta stared at the girls and then forced a grin.

"Oh, hi! I'm Shasta Sienna!" Shasta greeted them. She nodded at Rosie and added, "And this is Rosie—"

"Your stunt double," George finished. "Yeah, we heard."

"We thought you did your own stunts, Shasta," Nancy said.

Shasta gulped. She tossed her blue hair and laughed. "Rosie isn't my stunt double!" Shasta declared. "She's just a Glam Girl wannabe!"

"Wannabe?" Rosie cried.

Nancy watched as Rosie stormed away around the trailer. Shasta then flashed another superstar smile. . . .

"As if Rosie could ever be Glam Girl, right?" Shasta laughed. "See you girls later . . . when it will be lights, cameras . . . *me*!"

Nancy, Bess, and George watched wide-eyed

as Shasta disappeared into her trailer.

"You mean lights, cameras—diva!" George said, rolling her eyes. "Now can we please go to the sign-up table once and for all?"

Nancy, Bess, and George headed back to the table to hand in their permission slips. When all the slips were in, a woman named Melanie Chang introduced herself as the movie director.

"Please place your bags or backpacks on the side of the playground," Melanie announced with a smile. "We don't want anything to get in Glam Girl's way while she's chasing villains!"

Next, Melanie directed the kids to their places for the first scene. The girls were happy to be on the monkey bars. Also on the monkey bars was Lillian Lasko from the second grade at school. She wore a bright-red T-shirt that read RUNT RUN in white letters.

"What's a Runt Run?" Nancy asked.

"It's a race for kids tomorrow on Main Street," Lillian explained. "I'm running with the seven-year-olds!" Lillian smiled proudly as she added,

"They gave us this T-shirt and a backpack that I just put with the other backpacks. Now all I need is a new pair of running shoes—"

"Shh!" George cut in. "Melanie is going to speak!"

Nancy, Bess, and George listened to Melanie as she pointed out the movie equipment. Nancy's favorite was a camera set atop a crane for getting sky-high shots.

"Where are the lights?" a boy called out.

"Up in the sky!" Melanie said, pointing to the sun. "We're using natural daylight for this scene, so we're glad it's sunny today!"

After introducing the producer, makeup artist, and sound engineer, Melanie shouted, "Now for our star, Shasta Sienna—best known as Glam Girl!"

Nancy, Bess, and George cheered with the others as Shasta ran onto the playground. This time the blue boots shimmered on her feet.

"Hey, kids!" Shasta shouted. "Are you all ready to be stars just like me?"

"Give me a break," George muttered.

But Nancy and Bess shrieked, "Yesssss!!!"

Melanie gave Shasta her directions. She then turned to the kids for theirs. "When I say 'action,' everybody play and have fun," Melanie directed. "You can swing, slide, climb, talk softly to one another—just don't look at Glam Girl!"

"Don't look at Glam Girl?" Nancy whispered. "That's going to be hard!"

"Especially with cool boots like that," Lillian agreed. "Do you think they're really *super*boots?"

"They *are* for Glam Girl!" Bess remarked.

A hush fell over the playground until Melanie called, "Places . . . and action!"

Nancy and Bess scurried up the monkey bars. George flipped over one bar, swinging by her knees.

From the corner of her eye, Nancy could see Glam Girl walking across the playground.

"What do you mean Dick Dowdy has taken over Chic City?" Glam Girl said into a phone. "Don't worry—I'm on my way!"

Glam Girl dropped the phone into her pocket.

She then clenched her fists and froze in a running pose.

"And cut!" Melanie shouted.

Glam Girl turned back into Shasta as she whined, "It's about time. These boots are killing my feet!"

Shasta pulled off the blue boots and groaned, "I need a tootsie-break!"

Shasta walked barefoot away from the boots. Suddenly, Nancy saw someone peek out from behind a tree. It was Paloma—and she was holding a phone.

"What's Paloma doing here?" Nancy asked Bess and George. "She said she was leaving."

Before Bess and George could answer, Melanie announced, "Shasta is taking a short break so she can rest her feet!"

"You mean so we can meet her!" a boy called out.

"Let's get her autograph!" another girl squealed.

In a flash, Shasta was surrounded by a mob of kids shouting her name.

"Let's meet Shasta too!" Nancy told Bess and George.

"We already met Shasta, Nancy," George complained as she and Bess followed. "And we didn't really like her."

"We like Glam Girl!" Bess told her cousin. "And that's what counts!"

The girls stood in line with the others, inching slowly toward Shasta. Just when they were only two kids away, Melanie ordered the extras back to their places. Nancy, Bess, and George were disappointed not to get Shasta's autograph, but they were excited to start filming again.

As Nancy, Bess, and George headed back to the monkey bars, they could hear Melanie talking to Shasta. . . .

"Shasta, put the boots back on," Melanie told the star. "It's eleven thirty, and I'd like to film this scene before our noon break."

"No can do, Melanie," Shasta said. She pointed to the spot where she left her boots. "My boots are gone."

Melanie blinked as she stared at the empty spot. "What do you mean gone?"

Melanie asked the crew if they knew what had happened to the boots, but they were clueless. Then Melanie turned to the kids.

"Did any of you see or take Glam Girl's boots?" Melanie asked. "This is very, very important."

Nancy, Bess, and George shook their heads. The other kids did too.

"Matt, don't we have another pair?" Melanie asked. "The exact same kind as the missing ones?"

"No," Matt said. "Those boots were custom made for Shasta's feet. There's just one pair in the whole world!"

"Without Glam Girl's superboots," Melanie cried, "there is no movie!"

Nancy frowned. She had a feeling the blue boots weren't just gone—they were stolen. And to detectives like Nancy, Bess, and George that meant a mystery!

Chapter

3

SHOE CREW

"What do you think happened to the boots?" George asked.

"I think someone took them!" Nancy said.

"Who would want to take Glam Girl's boots?" Bess asked, waving her arms. "She's the star of the movie!"

Melanie called for everyone's attention. This time she spoke through an electronic bullhorn so her voice echoed through the playground. "If Glam Girl's boots are not returned by tomorrow afternoon, we'll be leaving River Heights for our next location."

Gasps and groans filled the air.

"Bummer," George said.

"Bummer is right!" Bess wailed as they went to pick up their backpacks. "Now we'll never be in a Glam Girl movie!"

Nancy didn't like the word "never." That's why she tried never to use it.

"Who says we won't?" Nancy said. "Glam Girl may have power clothes, but I have something just as good."

"What?" Bess asked.

"My power Clue Book!" Nancy said. She then reached into her backpack and pulled out her Clue Book with a smile. "Now, let's get to work!"

Tucked inside Nancy's Clue Book was her favorite pencil with the cool cupcake eraser on the end. She turned to a fresh page and wrote: "Who Took Glam Girl's Boots?" Then skipping two lines Nancy began their suspect list.

"I saw Paloma right before the boots went

missing," Nancy said. "She was holding a phone and looking straight at the boots."

"Paloma wanted the boots more than anything," Bess said. "She said they were the perfect blue for the fashion show tomorrow!"

"Remember how mad Paloma was when she couldn't borrow them?" George asked. "Maybe she was mad enough to take the boots!"

Nancy wrote Paloma's name in her Clue Book and then said, "Who could be suspect number two?"

"Someone who's mad at Shasta," Bess suggested.

Nancy's eyes grew big as she remembered Rosie, Shasta's secret stunt double.

"Rosie was mad at Shasta for telling her to hide," Nancy said.

"And for calling her a Glam Girl wannabe!" Bess remembered. "Not cool!"

But George shook her head. "I don't think it was Rosie."

"How come?" Bess asked.

"As Melanie said, no boots, no movie," George explained. "Why would Rosie want to lose her job?"

Nancy agreed. If Rosie was a stunt double, taking Shasta's boots would be the dumbest stunt of all!

"Why don't we look for Paloma," Nancy said as she closed her Clue Book, "and see if she pulled off the perfect crime?"

The movie crew was taking a break as Nancy, Bess, and George headed out of Turtle Shell Playground. Just then they saw a woman with bright blue hair carrying a gym bag.

"You guys, it's Rosie," Bess whispered, "Shasta's stunt double!"

"How do you know it's not Shasta?" George asked. "They look totally alike."

"Rosie's name is stitched on her gym bag," Bess said, nodding at the big red bag. "See?"

Nancy did see the name ROSIE ALVAREZ stitched on to the bag's outside pocket. But as Nancy looked closer she saw something else. Through the pocket she could see the outline of what was stuffed inside. And it looked just like—

"Boots!" Nancy gasped.

Chapter

BOOT CAMP

To get a better look Nancy, Bess, and George inched a few feet behind Rosie. When Rosie stopped to talk to a cameraman, they ducked behind a tall production trunk and listened. . . .

"We're going to grab some pizza, Rosie," the cameraman was saying. "Do you want to join us?"

"Can't, Dave," Rosie replied. "I'm the guest stunt double at Camp Daredevil this afternoon. I'm demonstrating stunts and signing autographs."

Nancy peeked out from behind the trunk. She

could see how surprised the cameraman looked.

"You signing autographs instead of Shasta?" the cameraman snorted. "What would she say if she found out?"

"I'm not telling the kids I'm Shasta's stunt double," Rosie insisted. "Besides, with those boots gone, I don't think we'll be seeing Shasta anytime soon."

Nancy, Bess, and George exchanged stunned looks.

"Rosie just mentioned Shasta's missing boots," Nancy whispered. "The same boots that might be in her bag!"

Peeking out again, the girls saw Rosie jump on a bike and pedal away.

"Rosie's on her way to Camp Daredevil," Nancy said as they stepped out from behind the trunk.

"What is Camp Daredevil, anyway?" Bess asked.

"It's a brand-new stunt day camp here in River Heights," George explained, "where kids learn to do things that look dangerous in the movies!"

"Dangerous?" Bess said, making a face. "I'd rather roast marshmallows and sing goofy camp songs."

"I think we should follow Rosie to Camp Daredevil," Nancy suggested. "It's right up the hill from here."

"Let's do it!" George said with a nod.

All three girls had the same rules. They could walk anywhere as long as it was five blocks or less away from their houses. And as long as they walked together.

"Okay, but what will we do when we get there?" Bess asked as they began walking up the hill.

"We will look for Rosie's gym bag," Nancy said. "Then we'll take a peek inside for the missing boots!"

Nancy, Bess, and George climbed the hill to Camp Daredevil. As they walked through the gate, they didn't see Rosie. Instead, they saw Peter Patino and Andrea Wu, two kids from their class at school. Both were wearing green-and-white Camp Daredevil T-shirts.

"Hi, Peter! Hi, Andrea," Nancy said. "I didn't know you went to Camp Daredevil."

"Sure we do!" Peter said with a grin. "Where else would we learn how to do this?"

The girls watched as Peter and Andrea performed some awesome forward rolls.

"Ta-da!" Andrea sang as the two sprang to their feet.

"Pretty cool," George admitted. "Now tell us where we can find the movie stunt pro, Rosie Alvarez."

Andrea pointed in the distance and said, "We heard Rosie's going to be at the Extreme Team Obstacle Course."

"Whoever runs through the course gets Rosie's autograph at the other end," Peter explained.

"How come you're not at the obstacle course?" Nancy asked.

"Can't," Peter said. "We've got our walking-over-poisonous-rattlesnakes workshop in five minutes."

"You're kidding me, right?" George asked.

"Maybe," Peter replied with a grin as he and Andrea walked away.

"Walking over rattlesnakes!" Bess shuddered. "I'll bet they drink bug juice made with real bugs too!"

"Forget about it," Nancy said. "Let's find that obstacle course and Rosie."

Nancy, Bess, and George made their way through Camp Daredevil, which looked like many day camps. There was a swimming pool, a tennis court, and a long log cabin with cooking smells drifting from the windows.

"I'll bet that's the mess hall," Nancy guessed, "where the campers eat lunch."

"And drink real bug juice!" Bess blurted.

"Let it go, Bess!" George said with a sigh.

The girls found a wooden sign shaped like an arrow, which read EXTREME TEAM OBSTACLE COURSE. They walked in that direction until the obstacle course came into view.

"Cool!" George exclaimed.

The course was in a big grassy field and surrounded by a chain-link fence. It started with a five-foot climbing wall. Behind it was a skinny plastic tunnel to crawl through. Next up was a rope to swing over a wading pool. The pool was filled with plastic blow-up sharks and alligators.

Last but not least was a playhouse. Kids, all wearing Camp Daredevil T-shirts, laughed and cheered as they jumped off the roof onto a cushy air bag.

"We found the obstacle course," George said. "But where's Rosie?"

Nancy looked beyond the course to see Rosie at the other side. As campers finished the course, Rosie autographed pictures of herself with a smile.

"There's Rosie," Nancy pointed out.

"And there's her gym bag!" Bess said.

Nancy looked to see where Bess was pointing. A few feet behind Rosie was her bike propped against a tree. Hanging from the handlebars was the suspicious gym bag!

"How will we look inside the bag?" George asked. "The only way there is—through the obstacle course."

"And we're not going to do that!" Bess insisted. "No way am I swinging on a rope over alligators and jumping off a roof!"

"They're toy alligators, Bess!" Nancy said, "And you'll be jumping off a playhouse onto a giant pillow."

Bess folded her arms across her chest and said, "I don't wanna!"

"I know the real reason why!" George snapped. "You don't want to mess up your new summer clothes—"

"Hey!" someone cut in. "You're holding up the others."

Huh? Nancy, Bess, and George turned to see a line of campers had formed behind them.

"You think we can do this before Christmas?" one girl quipped.

Nancy turned to her friends and whispered, "We have to see what's in Rosie's bag—so let's do it."

The three friends ran to the wall and climbed it together.

"I already got my blouse dirty!" Bess wailed. "This isn't an obstacle course—it's a slob-stacle course!"

When all three girls were over the wall, they crawled one by one through the tunnel.

"Woo-hoo!" Nancy cheered as she swung on the rope over the wading pool. "This is neat!"

While Bess and George took turns swinging on the rope, Nancy scrambled up the playhouse ladder. Up on the roof she made her way to the edge. But when she looked down she froze. The playhouse was higher than she had thought!

"Nancy, jump on the air bag!" Bess called as she and George climbed the ladder too.

"I can't!" Nancy squeaked.

Before Nancy could explain, a boy below pointed up and shouted, "That girl's not wearing a Camp Daredevil shirt. I bet she's not a camper here!"

Nancy gulped. They couldn't get thrown out of Camp Daredevil. Not before they checked out Rosie's bag!

"Sure I am!" Nancy shouted back. "Where else would I learn to do this?"

Throwing back her shoulders, Nancy gathered her Glam Girl courage. She then sucked in her breath, shut her eyes, and jumped!

Chapter

SPRING THING

"Whoooooaaaa!" Nancy shouted before landing on the air bag with a—*PLOOF!*

The bag gave a hissing sound as Nancy sank safely into it with a smile. She did it!

"I'm next!" George called.

Nancy rolled off the air bag in time for George to land. Next came Bess, this time smiling all the way.

"That was awesome!" Bess said. "Even if I did get my clothes dirty!"

"Speaking of clothes," George said. "Let's look in Rosie's bag for those boots!"

Nancy, Bess, and George left the obstacle course. Instead of going straight to Rosie, they slipped past the others toward her bike. The gym bag was still hanging from the handlebars.

"We can't let Rosie see us," Nancy whispered as she dragged the gym bag behind the tree.

Nancy unzipped the side pocket. She reached inside. What she pulled out made all three girls gasp: two blue boots!

"It's them! It's them!" Nancy said excitedly. "It's Glam Girl's power boots from the movie!"

"I'll stuff them underneath my shirt," George decided. "Then we'll sneak them past Rosie and bring them straight to Melanie—"

"Wait!" Bess cut in. She kicked off her own shoes and grabbed the boots. "I want to try these awesome boots on first!"

Before Nancy or George could stop her, Bess was slipping her feet into Glam Girl's boots. When they were on, Bess said, "They feel a little . . . bouncy."

"Bouncy?" George asked.

Bess bounced up and down lightly in the boots until—*BOING*—she jumped high into the air!

"Bess!" George said, "What are you doing?"

"I'm jumping!" Bess cried as she bounced and bounced. "And I can't stop!"

Thinking fast, Bess gripped an overhead tree branch. It stopped her bouncing. And her dangling feet gave Nancy and George a good look at the boots!

"There are tiny springs on the soles," Nancy pointed out. "No wonder Bess jumped so high!"

"That's weird," George said. "I held Shasta's blue boots before—and they didn't have springs."

"They do now!" Bess complained. "Will somebody please help me down—?"

"Having fun, girls?" someone interrupted.

Nancy, Bess, and George turned their heads. Standing a few feet away was—

"Rosie!" Nancy gasped.

"What are you doing here?" George asked.

"I needed to get more pictures to sign from my gym bag," Rosie said, before nodding at Bess's feet. "Instead, I find three girls with my boots."

Nancy decided to tell Rosie the truth. "We're looking for Glam Girl's missing boots," Nancy said bravely. She pointed to Bess's feet. "These look just like them."

"Except for the springs," Bess murmured.

"What's up with that, Rosie?" George asked.

Rosie helped Bess to the ground and then said, "I brought my boots here to show the campers later."

"*Your* boots?" George asked. "I thought they were made for Shasta's feet!"

"These boots were made for my feet," Rosie explained. "The springs help me jump high when I'm performing stunts."

"You mean they're not Shasta's?" Bess asked as she pulled off the boots one by one.

"Did you think I took Shasta's boots?" Rosie asked, wrinkling her nose. "Why would I do that?"

"You were mad at Shasta for calling you a Glam Girl wannabe," Nancy explained.

"Shasta wanted you to hide, too," George added. "I'd say that's a motive."

"A motive is a reason for doing something," Bess explained. "When we're not movie extras, we're detectives."

"Good for you!" Rosie said with a smile as she picked up the boots. "But Shasta says mean stuff like that to me all the time."

"That's not cool!" Nancy insisted.

"I know." Rosie sighed. "I do a lot of stunts—but my best one is ignoring Shasta when she's mean."

Nancy saw George tilt her head as if she was looking inside one boot. What was she looking for?

"Now that I have my gym bag back," Rosie said cheerily. "Would you like my autograph too?"

"Yes, please!" Nancy, Bess, and George chorused.

Rosie gave each girl an autographed picture of herself performing a stunt. She wasn't dressed like Glam Girl in the picture, and Nancy wasn't surprised. Being Shasta's stunt double was Rosie's biggest secret!

Nancy, Bess, and George thanked Rosie and then headed out of Camp Daredevil.

"What were you looking for inside those boots, George?" Nancy asked.

"The size!" George explained. "Those boots were size eight and a half. Matt told us that Shasta's boots are size six."

"That's a big difference," Nancy agreed.

"Are we looking for Glam Girl's boots?" Bess teased. "Or Cinderella's glass slipper?"

The Clue Crew had ruled out Rosie. But they still had another important suspect to consider: Paloma Garva.

"If Paloma has Glam Girl's boots, she'll be wearing them to the fashion show tomorrow," Nancy said as they walked home. "We have to go too!"

"To a real-live fashion show?" Bess said excitedly.

"I'd rather go to the dentist," George muttered.

Nancy smiled at her friends. She knew they would find some clues tomorrow at the fashion show. But time was running out!

"Don't forget, Daddy and Hannah," Nancy said that evening. "I want extra cheese and pepperoni on my slice and no anchovies!"

Nancy smiled at the thought of her favorite pizza toppings. After a full day of moviemaking and detective work, she was glad when her dad surprised her and Hannah with a trip to the pizza parlor.

"No anchovies?" Hannah teased. "You mean you don't like hairy little fish on your pizza?"

"I don't think so, Hannah." Nancy giggled.

Hannah Gruen was the Drews' housekeeper,

and she was great at making Nancy giggle. She was also almost a mother to Nancy since Nancy was only three years old!

"No anchovies!" Mr. Drew promised Nancy. "Why don't you grab a booth while Hannah and I order the pizzas and drinks?"

"On it, Daddy!" Nancy said.

Right away she found an empty booth and slipped inside. Sitting on the high-backed leather seat, Nancy took a whiff of the yummy-smelling pizzas in the ovens.

Maybe when I'm older, I'll try anchovies, Nancy thought. *But right now, I'll have to shut my eyes and squeeze my nose.*

Nancy's thoughts were interrupted by laughter coming from the next booth. The voices sounded like kids.

"This is the most awesome pizza celebration we've ever had!" a girl was saying.

"We deserve it!" a boy boomed. "The Popcorn Peeps have lots to celebrate!"

Nancy recognized the voice. It was Sidney

Schacter, but what were they celebrating? Leaning back further, Nancy listened in.

"It's about time we got something from a real-live movie set for our museum!" Sidney declared.

"Yeah!" another boy said. "Something big and blue!"

Nancy's eyes popped wide open. Did she just hear what she thought she heard? Did the Popcorn Peeps get something from a movie set?

Something *blue*?

Chapter

CLUE-SEUM!

Nancy tried not to make a sound as she listened to Sidney and his friends.

"It's a good thing you went to the Glam Girl movie shoot yesterday, Sidney," the girl said. "Just in time for our movie museum too!"

Nancy's jaw dropped. Their blue movie object was from the Glam Girl set. Could it be the missing boots?

Suddenly, Nancy heard the rustle of paper

plates and trays in the next booth. The Popcorn Peeps were leaving.

Nancy didn't want Sidney and his friends to know she was there secretly listening. So she sunk way down in her seat as they left the pizza parlor.

"Whoa!" Nancy whispered to herself. "I told Sidney to go to the Glam Girl set. But I never told him to take Glam Girl's boots!"

"One slice with pepperoni and extra-cheese and absolutely no little hairy fish!" Mr. Drew announced as he and Hannah approached the booth.

As they placed their trays on the table, Hannah asked, "Did we miss anything exciting?"

"Yes!" Nancy exclaimed with a nod. She pulled out her Clue Book and scribbled Sidney's name inside. "A brand-new suspect!"

"I am so hoping Sidney *did* take Glam Girl's boots," George said the next morning.

Nancy, Bess, and George were on their way to Sidney's house. They wanted to question him and check out his movie museum for the missing boots.

"Why, George?" Nancy asked.

"If we find the boots, I won't have to go that dumb fashion show this afternoon!" George said.

"Blah, blah, blah," Bess said. "Maybe you'll learn something—"

"You guys!" Nancy cut in. "Can we please talk about the case?"

"Sure," George agreed. "What's the plan?"

"Easy," Nancy said. "All we have to do is get into the Popcorn Peeps' museum. If the boots are there, we'll see them."

The Clue Crew found Sidney in his front yard. He wore a Popcorn Peeps T-shirt while tossing a Frisbee to his dog. The frisky yellow Labrador reminded Nancy of her own Lab, Chocolate Chip!

"Hi, Sidney!" Nancy greeted him, petting the dog after he scampered over. "Can we see your new movie museum?"

"Please?" George said, forcing a smile. "We've heard so much about it."

"Sorry," Sidney said, shaking his head. "The museum isn't open yet."

"Why not?" Bess asked.

"The Popcorn Peeps have to set up our excellent new attraction first," Sidney explained.

"Attraction, huh?" George said, rubbing her chin thoughtfully. "Could that attraction be something you got at the Glam Girl set yesterday? Something . . . blue?"

"My lips are zipped!" Sidney declared, running his fingers across his mouth. "And why would detectives suddenly be so interested in my movie museum?"

"Um . . . because we like detective movies?" Nancy answered quickly.

"Well, you've got to wait for opening day like everybody else," Sidney said. "Now if you'll excuse me, I have to walk Brando."

"Woof!" Brando barked.

While Sidney clipped a leash on Brando's collar, Nancy whispered, "We have to get inside that museum, but how?"

"I just thought of something," George whispered. "Watch this."

George pulled a folded piece of paper from her jeans pocket. As she unfolded it, Nancy saw what it was: Rosie's autographed picture from yesterday!

"Sidney Schacter," George said. "This is your lucky day!"

"How come?" Sidney asked.

"Because," George said, holding up the picture, "I have this for your new museum."

Sidney wrinkled his nose as he studied the picture. "Rosie Alvarez? Who's she?" he asked.

"Only the best stunt double that's ever lived!" George said.

"Yeah!" Bess said. "Nobody knows that Rosie is Shasta Sienna's stunt double—"

Bess stopped midsentence as Nancy clapped her hand over Bess's mouth. But it was too late . . .

"So Glam Girl has a stunt double, huh?" Sidney said, eyeing the picture. "Okay. We'll take it for the museum."

"Not so fast," George said. "We'll give it to you under one condition."

"What?" Sidney asked.

"That we put the picture inside the museum ourselves!" George said quickly. "We want to make sure it gets the best spot!"

"That's how special it is!" Nancy added, her hand still over Bess's mouth.

"You drive a hard bargain, but okay," Sidney finally agreed. "The museum is in the basement of my house. Just don't look behind the closet door."

Nancy wondered why not. But as Sidney led a frisky Brando out of the yard, George said, "We'll just look for the missing boots."

"Mmmph!" Bess tried to speak behind Nancy's hand.

Uncovering Bess's mouth, Nancy asked, "Why did you tell them about Shasta's stunt double, Bess? It was supposed to be a secret."

"I know, and I'm sorry!" Bess admitted. "Secrets sometimes spill out of my mouth—like milk when you're laughing."

"Forget about it," George said. "It got Sidney to let us into the museum, so let's get to work!"

Nancy, Bess, and George found the Schacters' basement door, leading to the museum. They opened the door and then climbed down into the dark basement.

Reaching along the wall, Nancy found the light switch. With a flick of the switch, the Popcorn Peeps' movie museum came into view. . . .

"Wow!" Nancy said, looking around the basement. Tables were set up along the walls filled with all kinds of stuff. Note cards explained what the items were. . . .

"More chewed-up gum in a jar," Nancy pointed out. "Scraped off from under a desk on the set of the TV show, *Cool School*."

"Not cool!" Bess cried. She pointed to a balled-up tissue on the table and asked, "What's that ewie thing?"

"Read the card, Bess," George said. "It's where the action star Will Gordon blew his nose."

"Blew his nose?" Bess cried. "This isn't a movie museum—it's a skeevy museum!"

Some not-gross items hung on the walls, like old colorful movie posters. On another table were hats, teddy bears, and cereal boxes that had been used as props in movies. There were boots but not the missing blue pair.

"Hey!" George said excitedly. "What's this?"

Nancy and Bess turned to see George holding a remote.

"George, there's no time for gadgets!" Bess said. "We have to look for the boots."

But George was already pressing the green button on the remote. After a few seconds—

WHIRRRRRRRRRR!

Nancy, Bess, and George traded curious looks.

"What was that noise?" Nancy asked.

"Where did it come from?" Bess asked.

"I don't know!" George said. She kept pressing the remote as the girls followed the sound. It seemed to be coming from behind a door.

"I'll bet that's the closet Sidney told us not to look inside!" Nancy said.

"Do we look inside or not?" Bess asked.

But before the girls could decide—

SLAM!!!

The door flung open and *"GROOWWWWLL!!"*

Nancy, Bess, and George froze. They stepped back as a big, blobby, and blue creature lumbered out of the closet.

"Omigosh!" Bess screamed. "What is it?"

"Whatever it is," Nancy cried. "It's coming for us!"

Chapter

CREATURE FEATURE

The blobby blue creature inched closer and closer, backing the girls against a wall. Nancy squeezed her eyes shut as the creature loomed menacingly over them. But just as she expected the worst—the whirring stopped.

Carefully, Nancy popped open one eye. The creature towered over them, his blobby arm frozen in the air.

"I pressed the red button on the remote, and it stopped," George explained. "It must be a robot!"

"A scary, giant robot!" Bess cried.

Sidney and two other kids charged down the staircase. Nancy recognized the kids as Nadine Nardo and Tommy Maron from their third grade class.

"Woof!" Brando barked as he shot down the stairs too. He took one look at the blobby creature and growled.

"Chill, Brando, chill!" Sidney shouted. He turned to Nancy, Bess, and George and said, "I told you not to look behind the closet door!"

Tommy grabbed a Martian-type blaster from a table. He pointed it at the girls and sneered, "Now we'll have to make you disappear, Earthling spies!"

"Speaking of 'Earth,'" Nancy said. She nodded at the blobby creature. "What on earth is *that*?"

"You've never heard of the Blue Blob Bot?" Sidney asked, holding Brando's collar tightly.

"Blue . . . Blob . . . Bot?" Bess asked.

"He's from the classic sci-fi movie *Invaders from Planet Gumball*," Nadine explained. "Tell him where you got it, Sid!"

"We went to Turtle Shell Playground yesterday for the Glam Girl shoot," Sidney said. "We wanted to pick up some souvenirs for our museum, but instead we talked to a guy named Larry."

"Who's Larry?" George asked.

"Larry worked as a real-live stagehand on the *Invaders from Planet Gumball* movie," Tommy said excitedly. "How cool is that?"

"Even cooler—Larry promised to lend us the real Blue Blob Bot for our museum opening!"

Sidney explained proudly. "He's had it in his garage for years!"

Nancy remembered Sidney and the Popcorn Peeps celebrating at the pizza parlor last night. Could they have been celebrating the Blue Blob Bot?

"Larry delivered the Blue Blob Bot yesterday afternoon," Nadine said.

"I put him in the closet so no one would see him before opening day," Sidney explained. "But thanks to you our secret is out!"

"We weren't looking for secrets," Nancy said, "just for Glam Girl's missing boots."

"We heard about the boots," Nadine said her eyes wide. "You don't think we took them, do you?"

"You did say you were at the movie shoot yesterday," George said. "Maybe you picked up more than a Blue Blob Bot!"

"That's what you think!" Sidney said. "Right after we talked to Larry, we went straight to my house."

"Larry told us *Invaders from Planet Gumball* was on TV," Tommy said, putting down the Martian-blaster. "We wanted to see the Blue Blob Bot we were getting for the museum."

Tommy grabbed the remote from George and said, "Watch how he spits blue slime too—"

"No, thank you!" Bess interrupted. She turned to Nancy and George and said, "Can we please get out of this gross place? Like, right now?"

Nancy didn't think Sidney and the Popcorn Peeps had the missing boots. So she smiled at Bess and said, "Sure."

"Wait!" Sidney said, folding his arms across his chest. "Aren't you forgetting something?"

"Oh . . . yeah," George said. She handed Sidney the picture of Rosie. Then the Clue Crew gladly climbed out of the cellar.

"I'm pretty sure the Popcorn Peeps didn't take the boots," Nancy said once they were outside.

"They just wanted that icky Blue Blob Bot," Bess agreed.

But George still wasn't so sure. . . . "Those

Popcorn Peeps could still have the boots," George said. "Boots aren't so hard to hide."

"They said they went home to watch the movie," Bess said. "I wish there was a way we could know for sure."

Nancy gave it some thought and smiled. "There *is* a way!" Nancy said. "Let's go to my house, and I'll show you."

The girls went straight to the Drew's house and Nancy's room. Nancy sat at her computer. Usually, George searched the web for clues, but this time Nancy knew what she was looking for: yesterday's TV schedule!

"The boots went missing around eleven thirty a.m. yesterday," Nancy remembered. "And yesterday's TV schedule has *Invaders from Planet Gumball* at eleven in the morning until half past noon."

"So, Sidney and the Peeps were watching TV when the boots went missing," Bess said. "Do you believe them now, George?"

"I guess," George sighed. "And I guess that

means we're going to that goofy fashion show to check out Paloma."

"For sure!" Bess said. "If Paloma took the boots, she'll be wearing them at the fashion show!"

Nancy pulled up the Girly Gear website to find out the time of the fashion show.

"It's at two o'clock," Nancy said. "We can still make it."

"Whoopie," George said, not smiling. She reached over Nancy's shoulder to point to the screen. "Look what else the Girly Gear website has. It's a video."

Nancy clicked on the video. On it excited girls chatted about the clothes they would wear in the fashion show. . . .

"Hi, I'm Amy!" one smiling girl said. "And I can't wait to show off my Girly Gear sundress and matching hat!"

"Hi, I'm Rachel!" another girl said. "I'll be modeling the most awesome Girly Gear shorts, top, and daisy statement necklace."

"Okay, this is boring," George said. She was

about to grab the mouse when Paloma appeared on the screen!

"I'm Paloma!" Paloma said. "My Girly Gear outfit is even more perfect with my brand-new perfectly matching blue boots. Come to the fashion show to see for yourself!"

"Did she just say blue boots?" Bess gasped.

"Sounds like a confession to me," George said. "What do you think, Nancy?"

Nancy narrowed her eyes at the frozen video image of a smiling Paloma.

"I think checking out Paloma's brand-new blue boots," Nancy said, "is the *perfect* plan!"

Chapter

CATTY CATWALK

Mr. Drew drove Nancy, Bess, and George to the mall. After parking, they rode the escalator straight up to the Girly Gear store.

"Remember, girls," Mr. Drew said. "Don't accuse Paloma of taking those boots too quickly."

"But Paloma was talking about perfect boots in the video, Daddy," Nancy said.

"That's what she called Glam Girl's boots when she first saw them, Mr. Drew," George added.

"Okay, okay." Mr. Drew sighed with a smile. "I'm just a lawyer, not a detective!"

When they reached the Girly Gear store on the second level, Bess exclaimed, "Neat! They have a real fashion runway!"

"I thought it was called a catwalk," George said.

"Maybe that's only for pet fashions," Nancy joked.

Guests were already seated for the show. Many of them were kids.

"The show starts in a half hour," Nancy said, looking at her watch. "We have time to find Paloma and question her."

"While you find Paloma," Mr. Drew said with a grin. "I'll find some coffee and a muffin."

"See you later, Daddy!" Nancy said.

The Clue Crew made their way to the Girly Gear entrance. A woman holding a clipboard and wearing a Girly Gear T-shirt stood at the door. The ID around her neck read ALLISON.

"Hello," Nancy said cheerily. "We'd like to go backstage at your fashion show."

"You can only go backstage if you're *in* the fashion show," Allison asked. "Are you girls models?"

Nancy stared sideways at Bess and George. They weren't expecting that question!

"Um . . . ," Nancy said.

"Er . . ." George hesitated.

Allison suddenly stared at Bess and smiled. "Isn't that a Girly Gear outfit you're wearing?" she asked.

"Um—probably!" Bess said quickly. She flashed the biggest smile ever. "Oh, and I can't wait to show it off in the fashion show!"

"Well, as the owner of Girly Gear, I am thrilled that you love our clothes!" Allison told Bess. "Hurry backstage with your friends and get ready for the show!"

"See?" Bess whispered as Allison led them backstage. "Being a fashionista comes in handy sometimes!"

Allison wished Bess good luck and then went

back to greeting people at the door. Nancy, Bess, and George looked around at the backstage excitement. A flurry of kids was getting ready for the fashion show. But where was Paloma?

Suddenly—

"This ponytail holder is perfect!" someone exclaimed.

The girls turned to see Paloma, gazing into a hand mirror. Nancy's eyes drifted down to Paloma's feet. That's when she gasped . . .

"You guys!" Nancy whispered. "Paloma is wearing blue boots with sparkly jewels!"

"Are they Shasta's boots?" Bess whispered.

"She's too far away to see!" Nancy said. "We have to get a closer look."

Before the girls could run toward Paloma, a man stopped them. The ID card around his neck read TREVOR TOWNSEND, HEAD HAIR HONCHO.

"You girls don't look like you've had your hair styled for the fashion show yet," Trevor said. "Have you?"

"Um, no," Nancy replied, "but—"

"Well, then," Trevor said, "go straight to the hair bar, and let my stylists work their magic!"

Nancy, Bess, and George traded worried looks. If they admitted they weren't in the fashion show, they might be told to leave. And they couldn't leave before checking out Paloma's boots.

"Okay," Nancy told Trevor.

"What do you mean 'okay'?" George whispered as they walked toward the hair bar. "I don't do barrettes. I don't do bows. And no way do I do glitter!"

"But I do it all!" Bess said excitedly. "Bring it!"

Nancy, Bess, and George sat side by side at the hair bar, which was a long table lined with mirrors. They waited quietly as stylists brushed, sprayed, and teased their hair, and then decorated it with all kinds of accessories.

By the time they were finished, Nancy's hair was brushed behind a purple headband, Bess's hair was braided, and George wore a barrette shaped like a pink butterfly.

"Pretty barrette, George," Bess remarked.

"It's yours," George said, handing it to Bess. "Now let's find Paloma, get the boots, and get out of here."

Paloma was still backstage. She was standing in front of a pink velvet curtain.

"Paloma!" Nancy called. "Can we talk to you?"

"Not now!" Paloma called back, before slipping through the curtain.

"Where'd she go?" Bess asked.

"There's only one way to find out," Nancy said.

The Clue Crew burst through the pink curtain. They hurried after Paloma until they looked around and froze.

"Cheese and crackers!" George exclaimed. "We're on the catwalk!"

Nancy looked to her left and then to her right. They *were* on the runway—and in the Girly Gear fashion show!

"What do we do?" Nancy asked.

"Pose!" Bess exclaimed.

"Give me a break," George groaned.

Nancy, Bess, and George followed Paloma on the runway, pretending to pose like supermodels. As the guests laughed, Paloma whirled around. When she saw Nancy, Bess, and George, her jaw dropped.

"Thank you, Paloma . . . and friends!" the announcer said.

Laughter still roared as Paloma, Nancy, Bess, and George walked through the curtain. When they were backstage, Paloma planted both hands on her hips.

"What were you thinking, following me on the runway?" Paloma demanded.

"What were you thinking, taking Shasta Sienna's boots?" George asked, pointing down at Paloma's feet.

"What?" Paloma cried.

"We saw you hanging around the Glam Girl movie set yesterday," Nancy explained. "You were looking at the boots right before they went missing."

"You really wanted the boots for the fashion show," George stated.

"How did you get grown-up boots to fit, Paloma?" Nancy asked. "Are you wearing five pairs of socks?"

With a roll of her eyes, Paloma said, "I have big feet for a kid. And these are not Shasta Sienna's boots!"

"They are too!" George insisted.

"Um . . . you guys," Bess said, staring down at Paloma's feet. "They're not."

Nancy stared at Bess. What did she mean?

Chapter

SHOE-IN SUSPECT

"What do you mean they're not, Bess?" Nancy whispered.

"Those boots look just like Shasta's!"

"Not totally," Bess whispered. "These boots don't have a yellow strip of fabric on top."

"So?" George asked.

"So, Shasta's boots did," Bess explained.

"Are you sure?" George asked.

"Have I ever been wrong when it comes to clothes?" Bess asked. "Well, have I?"

"Are you finished talking about my boots?" Paloma asked, tapping her foot impatiently.

"I have a question," Nancy said. "Where did you get boots that look just like Shasta's?"

"My uncle Sal is a shoemaker," Paloma explained. "I took a picture of Shasta's boots with my phone yesterday and showed it to him."

Nancy remembered Paloma holding her phone while eyeing Shasta's boots. So that's why she had a phone in her hand!

"Uncle Sal told me he could make boots that looked just like Glam Girl's!" Paloma explained. "And he made the perfect pair. See?"

Paloma turned to lift her foot. Stamped on the sole of her boot were the words BOOTS BY SALVATORE.

"That wasn't on Shasta's boots," George said.

Nancy nodded. There was proof that Paloma wasn't the boot thief—and the proof was in the boots!

"Sorry for thinking the boot-snatcher was you,

Paloma," Nancy said. "But we really want to find the missing boots so the movie can keep filming in River Heights."

"You probably know we're detectives," Bess added with a small smile. "We solve mysteries."

"Well, now you ruin fashion shows," Paloma cried. "Just like you ruined my perfect moment on the runway!"

"Paloma, guess what?" someone called.

All four girls whirled around. Walking over was Allison, a big smile on her face.

"Everybody loved your walk-on!" Allison said.

"Loved it?" Paloma said with surprise. She pointed to Nancy, Bess, and George. "Even with them following me?"

"The kids thought it was so funny," Allison exclaimed. "Now they all want the dress you were modeling!"

"Perfect!" Paloma exclaimed happily. She turned to Nancy, Bess, and George and said, "Thanks, you guys!"

Paloma turned back to Allison and said, "If

they liked the boots, my uncle Sal will make you the perfect deal!"

Paloma's and Allison's voices trailed off as the Clue Crew left Girly Gear. Nancy took out her Clue Book and scratched Paloma's name off her suspect list.

"Paloma is no longer a suspect." Nancy sighed.

"Neither is anybody else," Bess said. "We ran out of possible boot-snatchers."

Nancy looked around for her dad. She could see him on a bench, drinking coffee and reading something on his phone.

"Let's tell my dad we're finished with Paloma," Nancy said.

"Let's tell him we want to go home too," George said. "It's too late to find the missing boots."

"Too late?" Nancy asked.

"You heard what the director said," Bess agreed. "If the boots aren't found by this afternoon, the film crew is packing up and leaving River Heights."

Nancy frowned. She wasn't ready to pack up

her Clue Book. But Bess and George were right. Time was running out, and fast. Nancy was about to head toward her father when a boy walked over. He pulled a flier from a stack he was holding and handed it to Nancy.

"Don't forget about the Runt Run on Main Street today," the boy said. "First race is in half an hour!"

"The Runt Run," Nancy repeated as the boy walked on. "Isn't that the race Lillian said she'd be in today?"

"That's the one." George nodded. "I wonder if she got those new running shoes she wanted."

Nancy's eyes lit up as she remembered something else Lillian said at the movie shoot. It was about Glam Girl's superboots—and it was superimportant!

Clue Crew—and YOU!

It's your turn to solve the mystery of the missing boots! Think like the Clue Crew to solve the case, or turn the page to find the culprit!

1. So far the Clue Crew ruled out Rosie, Sidney, and Paloma. Can you think of some other boot-snatcher suspects? Write your answers on a sheet of paper.

2. Just when the Clue Crew thinks they ran out of suspects Nancy remembers Lillian. On a sheet of paper, list reasons why Lillian would want Glam Girl's boots. . . .

3. The Clue Crew is using their eyes and ears to solve the case. On a sheet of paper, write some other ways detectives might find clues.

Chapter

LUCKY STARS

"Nancy, what's the matter?" Bess asked.

"Yeah," George said, "your eyes are as huge as Frisbees!"

"Bess, George," Nancy said excitedly, "didn't Lillian wonder yesterday whether Glam Girl's boots were really magical superboots?"

"She did," Bess remembered too. "But I thought she was joking."

"Maybe she wasn't joking," Nancy said slowly.

George looked surprised as she asked, "Nancy,

are you thinking that Lillian Lasko stole the boots for the Runt Run?"

"Lillian did say she needed new shoes for the Runt Run," Nancy explained. "And I didn't see Lillian anywhere after we lined up for Shasta's autograph, did you?"

Bess and George shook their heads.

"That's when Shasta's boots were stolen!" Nancy pointed out.

"Even if Lillian did take Shasta's boots," Bess said, "How would she sneak them out of the park without anyone noticing?"

"I remember her saying she brought a backpack!" George blurted.

"Good enough!" Bess said. "Nancy, write Lillian's name in your Clue Book now!"

Nancy was about to pull out her Clue Book when Mr. Drew walked over. "How was the fashion show?" he asked. "Did you question Paloma?"

"Paloma is off our list, Mr. Drew," Bess said. "We have a new suspect now!"

"That's why we need to go Main Street right

away, Daddy," Nancy said. "Could you drive us there, please?"

"Don't you want to check out your favorite clothes stores first?" Mr. Drew asked.

"Thanks, Daddy," Nancy said. "But the only things we're interested in now are Lillian Lasko's boots!"

Mr. Drew drove Nancy, Bess, and George from the mall to a block near Main Street. Main Street itself was closed to traffic for the Runt Run.

"Remember," Mr. Drew said as the girls filed out of the car, "you can walk home as long as—"

"We walk together!" Nancy cut in with a smile. "Got it, Daddy!"

Mr. Drew drove off. The girls walked around the corner to Main Street. Crowds of people lined the sidewalk, cheering for the runners. Mayor Strong was there saying hi and shaking hands with the spectators.

Nancy, Bess, and George squeezed through the crowd to the curb. They looked down the block to see kids lining up at the starting line. A colorful sign propped up on a nearby easel read: NEXT RACE: SEVEN-YEAR-OLD SPARKS!

"Lillian is seven years old!" Bess pointed out.

Before the girls could look for Lillian, Mayor Strong stepped up to a microphone.

"Ready, Sparks?" Mayor Strong shouted with a smile. "Then on your mark . . . get set . . ."

"I still don't see Lillian!" Nancy said.

"Go!!!" Mayor Strong boomed.

Cheers filled the air as the seven-year-olds were off. Suddenly, Lillian burst through the crowd of runners. Her racing feet flashed brightly as she took the lead.

"Look!" Nancy cried as Lillian dashed by. "She's wearing boots. Blue sparkly boots!"

"What are we waiting for?" George shouted. "Let's go after her!"

Nancy, Bess, and George jumped off the curb and joined the race. But their eyes weren't on the balloon arch at the finish line. They were on Lillian and her boots!

"Lillian, wait up!" Nancy shouted.

When the kids in the crowd saw Nancy, Bess, and George, they began to shout too:

"Hey! I know those girls from school—and they're not seven!"

"Not fair!"

"Run with the eight-year-olds, posers!"

Lillian glanced back. When she saw Nancy, Bess, and George, her racing feet slowed to a skip. That's when another runner broke her stride to take first place!

"Oh, no you don't!" Lillian said as she picked up her pace.

The Clue Crew rocketed after Lillian.

"Lillian—wait!" Nancy called. Before they could catch up, Lillian darted under the balloon arch.

"Second place!" Lillian shouted happily. "That's faster than I ever ran before thanks to Glam Girl's magic boots!"

"Magic boots, huh?" Nancy asked as she, Bess, and George approached Lillian. When Lillian saw the girls, she gulped.

"Are those Shasta Sienna's missing boots, Lillian?" George asked.

"How can they be missing . . . when they're on my feet?" Lillian replied.

Bess pointed down at Lillian's boots and said, "Yellow shiny fabric at the top. They're the real deal!"

"Phooey," Lillian muttered under her breath.

Nancy was pretty sure Lillian took the boots. But she wanted to hear it from Lillian herself.

"Lillian?" Nancy asked gently. "Did you take Glam Girl's boots?"

"Okay, I did," Lillian confessed, "but I only wanted to run as fast as Glam Girl!"

"How were you able to run in grown-up boots?" Bess asked.

"They're small for grown-up boots!" Lillian said. "And I wore three pairs of socks to stuff them up."

George narrowed her eyes. "Well, dress-up time is over," she snapped. "It's time to return

* 85 *

those boots so the movie can stay in River Heights."

"Nuh-uuuuuh," Lillian said, shaking her head. "I'm going to keep these boots so I can win *every* race!"

"Those boots don't have superpowers, Lillian," Nancy explained. "You just thought they did, so you ran as fast as you could."

Lillian gave a little gasp. "You mean I can really run this fast? Even in my sneakers?"

"Probably faster," George said.

Lillian smiled as she pulled the boots off her feet. "Take the silly boots," she said. "They don't fit and all these socks are itchy!"

"What are you going to walk home in?" Bess asked.

"I left my sneakers on the sidewalk!" Lillian said. Her eyes lit up when she saw Mayor Strong walking over with a big silver trophy. "Wow! Who needs stuffy boots when you can have *that*?"

Lillian ran to get her second-place trophy. Nancy smiled as she picked up both boots.

"It's time for *us* to run now, Clue Crew," Nancy said. "Straight to the Glam Girl set!"

The Clue Crew ran like the wind to Turtle Shell Playground. The movie trucks and trailers seemed ready to roll out. Melanie Chang was about to climb into a truck when Nancy shouted, "Wait, Ms. Chang! Look what we found!"

When Melanie saw Nancy waving the boots in the air, she smiled from ear to ear.

"Are those the missing boots?" Melanie asked as the girls raced over. She turned and shouted, "Shasta, get over here quick!"

Shasta stepped out of another trailer. Then just like Cinderella she stepped inside the boots to see if they fit.

"Well?" Melanie asked hopefully.

"These are my boots," Shasta confirmed. "Pinchy toes and all."

"Now that we found the boots," Nancy asked. "Will you stay in River Heights?"

"I don't see why not!" Melanie said.

"Yes!" Nancy, Bess, and George cheered under

their breaths. They then took turns explaining how they found the boots on Lillian.

"I'm glad Lillian told you the truth," Melanie said. "And we're glad to have our star's boots back."

"Even if they do pinch," Shasta said. "So much for custom-made boots."

"At least they don't bounce." Bess giggled. "Like the ones with the springs on the soles."

"Rosie showed us how the stunt boots worked," George said. "Pretty cool stuff!"

Shasta stared at the girls. "So . . . you know the truth about Rosie?" she asked slowly.

"We're not the only ones," Bess admitted. "Some kids called the Popcorn Peeps know too because of me. Sorry."

"What we really know, Shasta, is that Rosie is not a Glam Girl wannabe," Nancy explained. "She's a hard-working stunt double who makes Glam Girl look strong and brave."

"Can't you be nicer to her from now on, Shasta?" Bess asked.

Shasta seemed to think about that. She then smiled and said, "Glam Girl shouldn't be a mean girl. From now on I promise to be nice to Rosie."

Nancy gave Shasta a thumbs-up sign.

"And I promise to give you girls bigger parts in the movie!" Melanie said. "How would you like to shout 'Go, Glam Girl' when she starts to run?"

"You mean we'll have lines?" Bess gasped.

"Like real movie stars?" Nancy exclaimed.

"We're ready for our close-ups!" George announced.

"I guess that means yes!" Melanie laughed. "Excuse us while we give the crew the good news."

As Melanie and Shasta walked away, the three best friends exchanged the biggest high fives ever.

"Great job, Clue Crew!" Nancy said. Then with a grin she pulled out her Clue Book and cupcake-eraser pencil and wrote the words, "Case closed!"

"Not only did we solve another case," George pointed out. "We're going to rock this movie!"

"So cool!" Nancy said excitedly. "And I think I really do believe in magic now."

"The magic of Glam Girl's boots?" Bess asked.

"The magic of movies!" Nancy replied happily. "Lights . . . cameras . . . *us*!"